Book Twelve

Contributing Authors

Springfield Public School- Mrs. B. Esler

Troy Giesbrecht

Casey Huigenbos

Abegail Sawatzky

Ella Spence

Taylor Telfer

Dagon Thibodeau

Liam Wall

Tyler Fehr

Mya Frampton

Vivian Goodwill

Travis MacIntyre

Kiersten Martens

Seth McGurran

Avery Musclow

Jett Plain

Nolan Shackelton

Landon Vantyghem

Liam Wilson

Contributing Authors

Davenport Public School- Mrs. Fleurie

Cadyn Hewbank	Mariah Pier
Megan Small	Lisa Braun
Morgan Kerr	Nevaeh Ball
Joel Zachary's	Joshua Klassen
Fisher Ward	Julian Green
James Porter	Austin Redekop
Evan Neustater	Chiquita Soules
Giuls Ierullo	Noah Smith
Sam Redekop	Benny Friesen
Austin Redekop	Diego Harder

Contributing Authors

Collegiate Avenue Public School- Mrs. Angela Hoffman

Ayden Ayles

Dea Bajramali

Rina Beka

Olivia Bolton

Ruben Dhillon

Reed Dobson

Ainslee Hannabuss

Chelsea J.

Adnan Kadric

Muziana Khan

Peyton Laird

Cora Little

Davin Ly

Teagan MacNeil

Rania Mahmood

Shakeel Mahmood

Sarah Malik

Nyasha Mandizadza

Levi McIntosh

Joudi Nabout

Lilyana Prokipczuk

Contributing Authors

Emily Stowe Public School- Donna Ross

Logan McLellan

Makendrah Shannon

Connor LaGro

Aiden Klassen

Jackson Avey

Abbigail Warboys

Brooke Hayes

Alivia Berrill

Lucie Panschow

Janneke Bos

Brooke White

Lucas Deamone

Genevieve McAllister

Contributing Authors

Davenport Public School- Miss Beth Buchanan

Ashley Shea

Alan Wall

Rayya McLeod

Ruben Quiring

Sienna Pratt

Holden Gibbons

Nathan Killins

ACKNOWLEDGMENTS

A very special thank you to all those who help make Write to Give happen. Each year, the program continues to grow and have a bigger impact on Canadian and international students. This would not happen, if it were not for the hard work of the teachers who have helped implement this program.

Thank you to our teachers, Miss Buchanan, Mrs. Ross, Mrs. Hoffman, Mrs. Fleurie, & Mrs. Esler!

Thank you to my team of editors, designers and family who have helped with W2G 2017.

Thank you,

Amy McLaren

A Sticky Situation, Eh?

Copyright © 2017

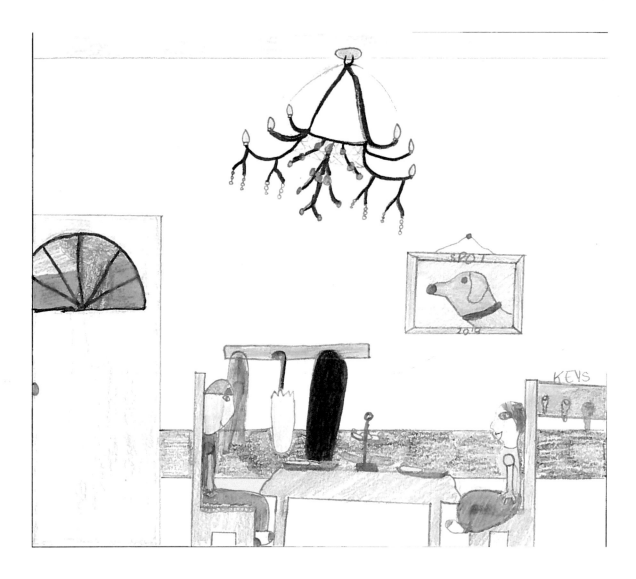

Zoey and Ryan were happy that it was finally the weekend. They were sitting at the table eating sausages and French toast.

They were trying to decide how to spend the day. They had been indoors most of the week. It had been raining.

Today the sun was shining and they were excited!

Hey Ryan, do you want to go to the park and play hide and go seek?"

"Yes, that's awesome."

They rushed to clean up and get ready to go. They filled their water bottles, grabbed some snacks and headed out the door.

"Do you want to take our bikes, Zoey?"

"No, let's enjoy the walk."

"I wonder if we will see any ducks at the pond?" asked Ryan.

"Maybe we will see some squirrels or chipmunks," replied Zoey.

The path into the park was mucky from the rain. The sky was blue and the air smelled like spring.

When Zoey and Ryan arrived at the park, they went into the forest to play hide and seek. Ryan was the first to count. Zoey bolted into a cluster of bushes and maple trees. As Zoey crouched into the bushes, she caught a glimpse of a small wooden shack.

As the sweet scent of savory maple syrup filled her nose, she realized it must be a sugar shack. That is when she heard the thump of a click-clack and the loud shattering of glass!

Cautiously, Zoey approached the shack with new suspicions in each step. She carefully opened the creaking wooden door, only to come face to face with large emerald green eyes and caramel-coloured fur.

Frozen with shock, Zoey caught her breath and screamed, "MOOSE!"

Ryan heard Zoey's distress and came running to the rescue, only to find his sister face to face with a 1000-pound moose.

Frozen with shock and fear, Zoey and Ryan stool while their hearts pounded.

The moose then tilted its head and said, "What's up eh?"

Zoey and Ryan quickly looked at each other in surprise. "A talking moose!" shouted Ryan.

"Thank goodness you're here to help me get out of this place! I've been living off maple syrup for days!" the moose exclaimed.

"Really?" asked Zoey.

"Well, when I smelled the sweet scent of maple syrup I came in the back door but my antlers kept getting stuck and breaking the windows." replied the moose.

"Maybe we can help you!" offered Zoey.

Ryan suddenly had a great idea. "Put your head down." The moose did just that.

"We can hold on to your antlers and guide you out of here."

Zoey and Ryan each took a hold of an antler. Carefully they led the moose safely out of the sugar shack.

"Thank you!" said the moose. "Do you have anything else to eat other than maple syrup?"

"We sure do!" replied Ryan and Zoey.

The brother and sister gave the moose some of their snacks that they had packed earlier. The moose particularly liked the jumbo carrots that the kids shared with him.

"Would you like to come home with us?" asked Zoey.

"I would love to but I have a family that I need to take care of" said the moose. "Why don't we meet at the sugar shack once a week to play hide and seek and eat jumbo carrots?"

Zoey and Ryan were so excited to have their very own talking moose as a friend.

The next week, Zoey and Ryan headed back to the forest and behind the sugar shack they spotted their friend the moose. He was with his family having fun.

The End

World Teacher Aid is a Canadian charity committed to improving education throughout the developing world with a focus on IDP settlements (Internally Displaced Persons – communities that have been uprooted from their homes). Our current projects are within Kenya and Ghana.

As a charity we are committed to providing access to education for students within settled IDP Camps. We accomplish this vision through the renovation and/or construction of schools.

Before we begin working with a community, we ensure that they are on board with the goal. A community must be settled and show leadership before we commit to a project. We also look for commitment from the Government, ensuring that if we step in and build the school, that they will help support the ongoing expenses, such as teachers salaries, and more.

AUTOGRAPHS

AUTOGRAPHS

Made in the USA
Middletown, DE
21 April 2017